THE PENGUIN BOOK OF

NAUGHTY POSTCARDS

GEORGINA HOWELL

PENGUIN BOOKS

Georgina Howell was born in South Africa in 1942. Her father served in the R.A.F. and they lived in Kimberley, London, the Midlands, the West Country, the North and Malaya. She left Miss Ironside's School in 1959 to take a full-time shorthand and typing course with journalism. In 1960 she won *Vogue*'s Talent Contest and joined *Vogue* as a copy-writer. She went to the *Observer* as fashion editor in 1965 and left two years later to have a son, Thomas. She has written *In Vogue*, a history of the magazine, which was published in 1976 by Allen Lane, and has lectured at the Victoria and Albert Museum on fashion.

Penguin Books Ltd, Harmondsworth,
Middlesex, England
Penguin Books, 625 Madison Avenue,
New York, New York 10022, U.S.A.
Penguin Books Australia Ltd, Ringwood,
Victoria, Australia
Penguin Books Canada Ltd, 2801 John Street,
Markham, Ontario, Canada L3R 1B4
Penguin Books (N.Z.) Ltd, 182–190 Wairau Road,
Auckland 10, New Zealand

Published in Penguin Books 1977

**Made and printed in Great Britain by
Ladybird Books Ltd, Loughborough**

INTRODUCTION

British comic cards are almost always naughty, not dirty, and if occasionally you come across a dirty one, it's seldom comic. The intention behind the two categories is different. Naughty postcards are like party blowers that unroll with a squeak and a feather – few people could take offence at them. Dirty postcards, however mild, take themselves seriously. The comic postcard's strength lies in its ambiguity. Most of the jokes are as old as civilization, but it's the difference between what you expect and what you get that still has the power to make you laugh. It's a point that was illustrated by Charlie Chaplin when an interviewer asked, 'How do you make an old chestnut funny again? For instance, the one about the pedestrian and the open manhole?' and he replied, 'There's an open manhole, and a man in a top hat. He walks along the road reading a newspaper, steps neatly over the manhole – and slips on a banana skin.'

Abroad, the distinction was not so easy to make. The first comic postcards were probably Prussian – an 1870 series of humorous designs coupled with suggestive verses – but France, with its *fin de siècle* reputation for the naughtiest nightlife in Europe, was soon known for its libertine cards. These principally featured 'French actresses' in various stages of undress, or more respectable but winsomely saccharine portraits of girls, many with a sentiment written underneath. One card showing a heavy girl picking roses and printed 'Je n'ai jamais aimé que vous' has a dozen kisses scrawled across the back and 'Chère Horase envoiyer carte photo a moi Julliette' [*sic*]. Hot stuff like this sent thousands of tourists visiting the Paris Exhibition of 1900 in search of naughty French postcards. The French government, however, was touchy: the post office had just issued instructions to its employees forbidding them (a) to read postcard messages, and (b) to forward any card bearing written insults or abusive expressions, including, presumably, heavy sexual innuendo. To protect the reputation of France, the Paris police made a series of raids on kiosks and tobacco shops where visitors to the 1900 exhibition might go, and confiscated 80,000 cards – among them, perhaps, the lavatory humour category, still a favourite French theme today. In Britain, three years later, a P. G. Huardel was summoned to Bow Street after his stock of 27,000 cards 'of continental origin' had been seized by the police: these, of ladies in négligées and bathing costumes, would be considered charming today. Nevertheless, many naughty cards got through the Edwardian post and the message on the back

Four cards of the kind seized by the police in 1903

was adapted accordingly: 'Excuse this somewhat vulgar card. It's one I had given needless to say,' to a Miss Robinson, and 'How are you blowing "Old Dear"? Love Charlie's Aunt', to a Mr Earnest Smith.

In 1902 the British post office took the initiative in allowing the whole of the front of the postcard to be printed with a picture, and the back to carry both message and address. By 1908 860,000,000 cards were being sent and delivered annually. Some were of the wasp-waisted heroines of the musical comedy stage, some the Bamforth cards illustrating hymns or popular songs, some the early comic cards by Charles Dana Gibson, Tom Browne, Louis Wain or Phil May.

In the eighteenth century, the seaside was a place for adult leisure, for improving the health, playing cards, dancing at subscription balls and flirting: the children were usually left at home with the servants. From the early days of Victoria's reign, with the growth of the railways, the seaside was mainly for children, even for poor children, and by the 1890s lodging houses were packed out with families who often came on holidays with their neighbours, to spend their days on the beach and their evenings playing games, singing round the piano, and eating and drinking together.

The first people to send naughty postcards in this country were the Edies and Arthurs who wrote from Ramsgate and Clacton in the first years of this century. When you consider what everyday work meant then, it's easy to see that a precious few days off were a good enough reason for high spirits, and that when millions of holiday-makers took a minute to scrawl 'Having a great time' on the back of a cheerful card, they meant what they said. Here, for instance, is the day of a house-parlourmaid employed in a small town house, set out by Mrs Dorothy Peel in *How to Keep House*, published in 1902:

Down 6.30; do drawing-room and morning-room (gas fire in latter); get breakfast for 8 (a.m.); have own breakfast; go up to bedrooms, do bedroom work and cleaning till 11.30; wash breakfast things and do knives; dress; lay and serve lunch; see to fires; have own dinner; clear lunch and wash up; do pantry work; needlework; answer door-bell; take tea; shut up sitting rooms; ring dressing gong; set table; see to fires and tidy up drawing room; serve dinner; clear, wash up; bed at 10.

Estimated annual salary: £15.

They usually wrote on the backs of cards that were gently naughty in the tradition of the music hall, relying on the pun and the *double entendre* – a phrase that might have been invented by the British rather than the French.

'I visit this place every year,' says the lady.

'Are your stays long?'

'Sir! I thought you were a gentleman!'

It was an Edwardian convention in comic drawings that the woman towered over the man.

At first this was not intended as a derogatory comment: a statuesque woman was 'a fine woman' like the Gibson girl Camille Clifford, or the Gaiety girls. The couture house Lucile, which dressed all the top musical comedy stars, showed their clothes on 'glorious goddess-like girls'. Lady Duff Gordon, the woman behind Lucile, described one as 'five feet eleven inches of loveliness', another as 'six foot one inch of perfect symmetry', and said, 'Not one of them weighed much under eleven stone and several of them considerably more.' In comic drawings this convention, beginning with Charles Dana Gibson's cartoons of the well-grown American heiress being wooed by the shrivelled British nobleman, soon degenerated into the purposefully built wife and the small henpecked hus-

band: the eleven stone came to rest around the girth. 'My wife's joined the Suffrage Movement,' says a small man blacking the grate. 'I've suffered ever since!' 'By gum!' says a hefty Edwardian holiday-maker, 'I've put that much weight on they won't let me bathe – they say it would flood the town.'

If there was one place where people looked ridiculous, and didn't mind, it was the seaside, where you took off your clothes and cut a figure of sorts. The eighteenth- and nineteenth-century cartoon was a direct ancestor of comic postcard humour, for instance the 'Back-Side and Front View of a Modern Fine Lady or Swimming Venus at Ramsgate', 1805. Since Friar Tuck, and probably before, a fat figure has made the British public laugh. Even Jane Austen is guilty of this unkindness in *Persuasion*, when she describes substantial Mrs Musgrove's melancholy over the fate of her deceased son:

Personal size and mental sorrow have certainly no necessary proportions. A large bulky figure has as good a right to be in deep affliction, as the most graceful set of limbs in the world. But, fair or not fair, there are unbecoming conjunctions, which reason will patronise in vain, – which taste cannot tolerate, – which ridicule will seize.

One hundred and five years later, comic postcard artists were having a ball with men and women of Mrs Musgrove's proportions, aided and abetted by that extraordinary anachronism, the early 1920s' bathing costume. Backless and short-skirted cocktail dresses showed far more

of the body than the heavy jersey bathing dresses that were worn right up to 1925: these might be an elaborate wrap-over dress and baggy pants to the knee, or a petal skirt and embroidered knickerbockers worn over a brassière cum corset in rubber sheeting, with a turban on the head. Men now wore bathing trunks with singlet tops, or braces, rolled up trousers and a knotted handkerchief for a sunhat. In fact, post-war figures were slimmer than ever, what with wartime jobs for women, hockey and tennis, rationed butter and sugar, emphasis on dancing and the new serpentine dresses. Like the elaborate bathing dress, fatness was a concept only reluctantly relinquished by the comic postcard artist.

Fashion has always been the butt of comics, beginning this century with *Punch* cartoons and cards like the one below, from 1911: 'One D— thing after another'. The trousers are a second-

One D—— thing after another!

or third-rate copy of Poiret's pantaloon dress. 'No wonder Adam fell' is the caption as a man falls flat on his face while watching an elegant creature cross the road in a Merry Widow hat and a harem skirt split to show the ankles. In the twenties outraged husbands goggle at their wives' short skirts:

'You're wearing an awfully short skirt, Gladys.'
'Well, haven't I a perfect right?'
'Rather! And a peach of a left!'

Ultimately, the test of a new fashion is how the wearer looks. The point was made in a joke which appeared in a 1925 issue of *Punch*.

HUSBAND: 'Really, Laura, if these skirts get any shorter they'll be hardly decent.'
WIFE: 'My dear man, don't you understand? All skirts are decent, but not all legs.'

The thirties brought in another well-loved comic convention – the bright red polkadot silky dress, worn over 'frillies', suspenders and stockings, with permed hair, red lipstick and high-heeled shoes. Before the end of the twenties it was said that everything a woman wore could be cut out of seven yards of fabric, and that fabric was likely to be the new cheap rayon that printed well and felt like silk. The vamp of the comic postcard is so seldom seen out of this classic spotted red dress from the thirties onwards that she would be scarcely recognizable without it. In the same way, the wedge heels that provided the one glamorous device that postcard artists could add to their repertoire from the drab Utility wardrobes of the forties came to be regarded as part of a vamp's equipment and can be seen in comic cards for years afterwards. 1947 brought in Christian Dior's New Look, the biggest run-away success in the history of the trade, and the wasp waists and exaggerated breasts and hips made it a natural for the comic postcard industry too. 'She calls it her atomic dress,' says one boy to another. 'It's got 20% fallout.' And of the mini-skirt: 'They're still four inches below See Level.'

Postcards transformed the writing style of the public. In the first place, they put people in touch with each other quickly and easily. Many people who would not have bothered to write a laborious letter found time to scribble 'Arrived here safely. Having a good time' – non-messages that mean little to the outsider, but put many relations' minds at rest. There was no room for beating around the bush, just space to tell others they weren't forgotten while implying you were having no end of a time at Blackpool. Some cards are almost brutally to the point:

Dear Ma, Please will you get my other white coat from my old shop and send to me at *once* there is 6d. to pay for washing. Will return same. Received Parcel with Thanks Everything OK Love Arthur XX.
P.S. It has been scorching here today. Also send my other black shoes.

This card, sent as late as 1934, shows how reliable the post was, and how often people relied on the mail rather than the telephone. Although there were 775,000 telephones in Britain by 1914, there were also so many postal collections and deliveries that there was no need to have a phone. Anyone wanting to go to tea with a friend living in the same district had only to send a postcard by the morning's post to be sure they would be expected at four. Even in the 1890s, in *Diary of a Nobody*, Charles Pooter reprimands his son Lupin for proposing to send a wire to a friend to cancel the next day's visit. 'I suggested that a postcard or letter would reach her quite soon enough, and would not be so extravagant.'

The plain ha'penny postcard had been first issued ready-stamped on 1 October 1870. Later, the post office relinquished its monopoly on cards, and sold stamps separately. Nevertheless there were strict rules about where you wrote your message and where you stuck your stamp. The man who wrote

Hey diddle diddle
The stamp's in the middle.

had his card returned with a post office addition

Hey diddle dey
There's tuppence to pay!

The way we write cards is a fashion that has changed, chiefly, in becoming more self-

Keep the kettle boiling, Mary, while I'm away,
Don't you fret or worry, Mary, for you I'll pray;
I've got to do my duty far across the foam,
So keep the kettle boiling, dear, till I come marching
  home.

When the war ended Bamforth destroyed their stocks of 20 million sentimental cards such as 'Somewhere a heart is waiting' and 'In the misty land of someday', and they were never revived. The comic postcard changed less, and now seems less embarrassing than the serious card, with its straightforward misinterpretations of army life. For instance, a smiling soldier with a girl on each arm is captioned: 'I hear you're moving – trust the night will be a fine one.'

One sort of comic card had also disappeared, the kind that made fun of the miserable working-class marriage with the overbearing wife who feared sex because it meant children, and the husband who escaped to drink. Marriage is of course a perennial comic-card subject, but now middle-class marriage was laughed at too. The pre-war card that showed mother and father in bed with a row of children between them – 'He said "Nothing will ever come between us" But in five years they've drifted apart' – gave way to the Donald McGill showing a newly wed husband saying goodbye to his in-laws. 'Be careful old man,' says the father, 'and don't have any accidents.' 'Rather not,' says the young man, 'Can't afford any for a year or two!' Birth control clinics were seldom if ever used as a subject, though many recent postcards have been designed around the idea of the pill.

Comic artists avoided the many grim subjects that occupied people's lives and minds in the between-war years – the dole, the means test, the unemployment rate of 3 million – and concentrated on getting away from it all with cards featuring the new spiv and the smart girl who answered back in the language of the movies. It was a long way from the 1910 vamp sitting in the palm of a man's hand and captioned, 'I've got a nice little handful here,' to the self-confidence of the 1930s' girl – 'Is it time for the car to break down, George?'

Second World War postcards provided less sentiment and escape into mawkishness than had

conscious. The above is one of many examples of unintentional early humour in the collection of Richard Chopping. But the fact that everyone could read what you wrote could occasionally be turned to your advantage. Perhaps Edith Sitwell thought it too crude to make public a letter that she began: 'Dear Mrs Almer, After five years, you have again been kind enough to ask me to dinner . . .' We've often become quicker and wittier. It is interesting to compare messages on the backs of two postcards of shapely legs. In 1914 'Dear Alice, Arrived here safely. Having a good time just a snapshot of our legs not so bad.' In 1976 'Is this card unseemly?'

Postcards reflected the charged atmosphere of the First World War in two ways. Overwhelming sentiment and naïve patriotism revived the high-flown style of pre-war hymn cards. Simpering heroines posed by firesides above fatuous rhymes:

NERVOUS? —
NOT IN THESE TROUSERS!

IT'S A WRONG WAY TO TIP 'ER 'ARRY!

those of the First. There was nothing much worse than the smiling W A A F

> Keeping up the good work
> With a cheery smile,
> That's the spirit, girlie,
> You'll find it's well worth while!

The gap between the world of the servicemen and that of the civilians was not so wide as before. Not only was communication easier, but life at home was dangerous and uncomfortable, dirty and odd. Bombs, moving, camping in hotels or other peoples' houses, bicycling everywhere, queueing for everything became part of life, and the theme 'Are we downhearted?' was one that suited comedy best. 'If you haven't any coupons, what can you do?' asks a girl in bra, pants, stockings and muffler. Instead of cards of a misty-eyed girl keeping the home fires burning, there were cards showing a line-up of healthy, laughing women: 'A little present to the boys who are doing their bit! Take your pick, lads!'

It takes a war to alter the tone of a naughty postcard. The humour soon reverts to its natural course. New situations only provoke the old responses, and permissive generations look much the same as others in the distorting mirror of the comic card. Certain themes to be found in this book are of recurring interest: soon there should be a revival of Sultan and Arab jokes as London fills with oil sheiks. Through it all runs a thread of irony that makes the humour peculiarly British. We see ourselves looking ridiculous, and

"WHAT A-WAR!"
By Gilbert Wilkinson
With Acknowledgments to the "Daily Herald"

"Mock invasion practice, nonsense, I've got gout!"

OUR COUNTRY DID IT BEFORE AND WE ARE GOING TO HELP DO IT AGAIN!

English and American views of the war

we think, 'It's a great life if you don't weaken.'

Vulgarity and bawdiness have always been close to the hearts of English-speaking people, emerging in the early minstrel's songs and the music hall, in drinking songs and fourteenth-century limericks, in Shakespeare and the lines of stand-up television comedians, in Herrick and Eskimo Nell. If comic postcards should die out, the humour would surface again in some other form. Like the rhyme you hear children chant in the playground, no one knows where it comes from, but it's here to stay:

> We three kings of Leicester Square
> Selling ladies' underwear
> No elastic
> Quite fantastic
> Penny a pound a pair.

I CAN'T MAKE MY EYES BEHAVE. -

Waiting for the Smacks.

DON'T WORRY, EVERYTHING IS GOING ON ALL RIGHT.

AM FEELING AWFULLY
BUCKED!

"I LIKE YOUR CHEEK!"

THIS IS WHAT WE DO AT SOUTHEND

I feel an awfully giddy kipper amongst the dear little soles!

"There's nothing to be upset about because a man proposed to you!"
"Ah! But you don't know what he proposed!!"

"Look—both hands! Now will you believe it wasn't me?"

"I'm just going to look under the bed and
see if there's a marauder there."
"It's allright, Dear, — it's round this side!"

When the sun is riding high
 Her love is just platonic,
But, Oh, when the moon is in the sky
 And she's had a gin and tonic!

ALL THE GIRLS ARE LOVERLY LOVERLY.

ICI TOUT RESPIRE . . .

"Take this jelly away, Waiter. There are TWO things on this earth that I like firm and ONE of them's jelly!"

"OH, GO ON, DICK — THE FURTHER YOU'RE IN THE NICER IT FEELS!"

"YES, IT'S MY FIRST TIME HERE, AND I MUST ADMIT YOU HAVE A MOST ATTRACTIVE FRONT!"

"I hear you've got a groom at last." "Yes, I had to work like a horse to get him."

"THIS REMINDS ME, JACK IS DATING ME TO-NIGHT"

"YOU UNION MEN ARE ALL THE SAME — STICKING OUT UNTIL YOU GET WHAT YOU WANT!"

"IT'S ME, NOBBY!"

"AH, MR. MACTAVISH, I SEE YOU HAVE SOME GINGER NUTS."

"I wish I'd got a nice fat worm like that"

"The scenery's grand — you should see the lovely caravan sites here!"

THEY'RE OFF

We are enjoying the sea breezes at Ramsgate...

I SAW THESE HOBBLING ABOUT LAST NIGHT, ARE THEY YOURS?

HOW BRIDGET SERVED THE POTATOES UNDRESSED.
I'll not take off another stitch if I lose my place.

 ICKORY, DICKORY DOCK,
A MOUSE RUN UP THE CLOCK;
OH YOU'VE HEARD OF NOTHING SADDER
'CAUSE THE CLOCK WAS ON HER STOCK
AND THE MOUSE RAN UP THE LADDER.

" Your Mother never dressed like this, and
yet she found a husband."
Wife : " Yes, found him with my eyes shut."

"Did you ring Sir"

We aren't half seeing what goes on here.

I said "hands up," Miss, but please yerself—that's O.K. by me

"YOU'RE WEARING AN AWFULLY SHORT
SKIRT, GLADYS."
"WELL, HAVN'T I A PERFECT RIGHT?"
"RATHER! AND A PEACH OF A LEFT!"

"No, I'd better have the dark blue ones - - he's an Oxford man!"

"WHEN A BREEZE BLOWS UP, IT IS HARD FOR A GIRL TO COVER HER EMBARRASSMENT."

BEEN TROUBLED WI' WIND SINCE WE CAME HERE - - - THE SORT THAT GIN AND PEPPERMINT WON'T SHIFT

AT HASTINGS

"I see everything that goes on here!"

"I can show you something nice in nylons, Sir!"

"IT MAY BE A BULL OVER THERE. BETTER TAKE YOUR HAT AND THAT PAIR OF RED SHOES OFF!"

"Dammit, young lady, is it necessary to start at that infernal speed?"

"I HOPE YOU LIKE THIS FRILLY TRANSPARENT PAIR — LET ME TRY THEM ON YOU FOR SIZE."

"It's my little Rosie behind I
want photographed."

"Take your clothes off quick—
here's the wife coming!"

"I CAN'T KEEP IT UP FOR TWO HOURS!"

"TALK ABOUT PERSUASIVE! HE DID ME IN THREE DIFFERENT POSITIONS FOR HALF-A-CROWN"

"IS THAT ALL YOU'VE DONE WHILE I'VE BEEN OUT?"

"Gosh Mary, just look what happens when you have children!"

JUST MARRIED

"Be careful old man and don't have any accidents."
"Rather not - can't afford any for a year or two!"

"Are you nervous, darling?"
"Oh, no - I was never so cocksure"

"Quick dear, before it gets soft"

"JUST MARRIED—IT STICKS OUT A MILE!"

"I'm whacked!—Half the night it's been 'Up and Down'—'In and Out'—I swear I'll never book another room next to the lift!"

THE TRUE GOLFER!

"Yes I've been through once!"

"THERE'S A WORM IN THE BED!"

"A SECOND HONEYMOON?— WHO YA MARRYING?"

"I'LL HAVE A LEMONADE, COFFEE KEEPS ME AWAKE AT NIGHT!"

AND what are you doing in my bed?

UNDER THE DOCTOR

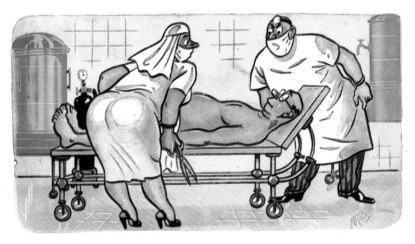

"BUT NURSE—I SAID REMOVE HIS SPECTACLES!"

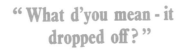

"What d'you mean - it dropped off?"

HOW I FELT BEFORE THE MEDICAL BOARD.

"Your mother-in-law ought to have a blood transfusion, but we can't find any in her group."
"Have you tried a TIGER'S, Doctor?"

"Come now Mrs. Johnson, a little prick won't hurt you!"

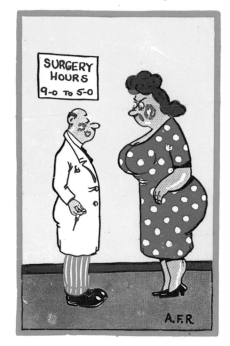

"THOSE BIRTH CONTROL PILLS YOU GAVE ME MUST BE TOO SMALL DOCTOR—THEY KEEP FALLING OUT!"

"WELL, NURSE — TAKE HIS BALLS OFF FIRST !"

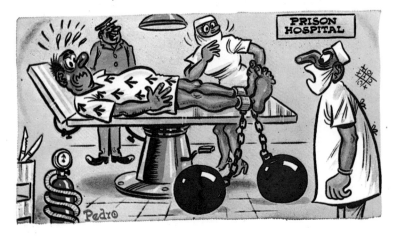

What the dickens Doc wants a sample of my water for, I am dashed if I know.

"WHEN DID I LAST HAVE RELATIONS, DOCTOR?"
"SIX MONTHS AGO, WHEN MY AUNT JANE CAME TO STAY"

"She'll be all right in a minute, she is only suffering from over-exposure!"

"THAT'S THE FIRST TIME I'VE HEARD IT CALLED A THERMOMETER - DOCTOR!"

"NO, NO, NURSE DUNCAN, I SAID PRICK HIS BOIL"

5

ON THE JOB

"**I'M** afraid your husband isn't in a position to see you at the moment!"

Heu... qu'es-ce que je disais ?

"My! My!—Hasn't he got a lovely big packet"

"IT'S NOT SO MUCH THE COFFEE— BUT I LIKE THE WAY SHE WIGGLES WHEN SHE GRINDS!"

"CARD FROM MY BOSS — ON HOLIDAY WITH HIS WIFE — SAYS HE'LL BE GLAD TO GET BACK TO THE DAILY GRIND!"

12087   "The pressure is getting too high, Mr. Flypip!"

"I'm all ready for you—try and get it up as far as you can!"

"Young man—I'd like a hand up here,
I want to get felt on the stairs first!"

Before you move that, will you come
upstairs and take my drawers down.

"FANCY BEING JEALOUS OF THE MILKMAN—HE'S IN AND OUT IN FIVE MINUTES!"

" Morning, Miss. Have you an opening for a young man with plenty of energy ! "

"IS THAT WHAT YOU GET PAID FOR?"
"NO GUV! I DO THIS FOR NOWT!"

UNDER THE FLAG

Mooning Series.

HER SOLDIER BOY.

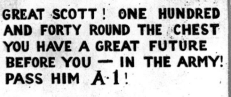

GREAT SCOTT! ONE HUNDRED AND FORTY ROUND THE CHEST YOU HAVE A GREAT FUTURE BEFORE YOU — IN THE ARMY! PASS HIM A 1!

FRED. SPURGIN

Si seulement j'étais
presentable !

AFTER A LONG MARCH, I'D LIKE
TO BE CLEANED AND PRESSED!

"What's the chance of some shore leave tonight, Captain?"

What rank was that sailor you were with last night?

I think he must have been the chief PETTING officer.

"SERGEANT BULSTRODE HAS THE BIGGEST PRIVATES IN THE REGIMENT."

"They all seem very erect!"

"WHAT A MAN YOU ARE!"
DON'T BE SILLY GIRL, THAT'S ME
TELESCOPE!"

LITTLE BASKETS

NOW THAT FATHER'S
SHAVED HIS WHISKERS OFF, AND
MOTHER WEARS A HAREM SKIRT,
HOW CAN I TELL WHICH IS WHICH?

"JUST PAID ANOTHER £5 OFF THE
DOCTOR'S BILL, DARLING."
"SPLENDID, JACK! TWO MORE
PAYMENTS AND THE BABY'S OURS!"

"Now, which of you is going to be Mother?"

"THE STORK HAS BROUGHT YOU A BABY BROTHER, JIMMY---WOULD YOU LIKE TO SEE HIM?"
"NO!---LET'S HAVE A LOOK AT THE STORK!"

A "BAMFORTH" COMIC

"IT'S NOT THE JOB THAT BOTHERS ME—IT'S ALL THE PAPERWORK AFTERWARDS."

"You naughty boy! You mustn't stick
    pins into Spiders!"
"Why not? You sew Buttons on Flies!"

"What, twins again, Mrs. Lovejoy! Do
    you always have twins?"
"Oh no, Vicar! Lots of times we don't
    have anything at all!!"

"It's so different from yours! Did his
father have nice curly hair like this?"
"I don't know, Ma'am, he had his hat on!"

"Oh Aunty! What a funny
place to keep the hairbrush"

"JUST LIKE HIS FATHER—HE'S A SUCKER FOR A LEFT—TOO!"

86

"It's funny how heavy this little basket gets!"

Mum said if I look at pictures like this I'll turn into stone.... I've started !

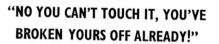

"LITTLE PERCY HOPES YOU'LL BE MY FAVOURITE MISTRESS TOO!"

"NO YOU CAN'T TOUCH IT, YOU'VE BROKEN YOURS OFF ALREADY!"

MUMMY, MUMMY, DADDY MUST HAVE SWALLOWED AN ELEPHANT — 'COS I CAN SEE IT'S TRUNK STICKING OUT!!

THEY KICKED HIM FROM THE NUDIST CLUB,
THEY DIDN'T SAY "GOOD-BYE,"
BECAUSE HE TURNED UP ON PARADE,
WEARING HIS OLD SCHOOL TIE!"

11936   He: "I am new here and glad
            to meet you."
        She: "Yes. I can see you are."

"I'M USED TO IT NOW, BUT THE FIRST THREE DAYS WERE
THE HARDEST."

"I ALWAYS WEAR A HAT—THEY'RE NOT FUSSY WHOSE NUTS THEY PINCH!"

"YOU SHOULD SEE THIS PLACE AT LOW TIDE!"

ARABIAN NIGHTS

"I GO THROUGH ABOUT FORTY A DAY!"

"My wife's about to become a mummy!"

"TURKISH OR VIRGINIAN?"

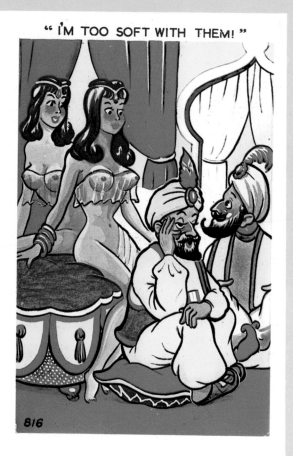

"I'M TOO SOFT WITH THEM!"

YOU **MUST** HAVE A COMPLETE REST — CAN YOU STAY OUT OF BED FOR A COUPLE OF WEEKS?

INDOOR GAMES AND OUTDOOR SPORTS

"If you do, George, I shall scream."

"WE'RE HAVING A MERRY TIME."

SISTER'S YOUNG MAN SAYS GOOD NIGHT.

When I showed Jane my little top,
She screamed out with delight.
Now she's so fond of " Put and Take "
We play it every night !

Hostess :—" Must you have teacups, can't you tell fortunes with cocktails ?"

"WHAT ABOUT CHANGING PLACES, GEORGE? THE VIEW FROM HERE IS GETTING RATHER MONOTONOUS."

"I'D FEEL SAFER, MR. MURGATROYD IF YOU SUPPORTED ME JUST A LITTLE FURTHER FORWARD."

I HOPE TO GO AROUND IN EVEN LESS TOMORROW JOHN!

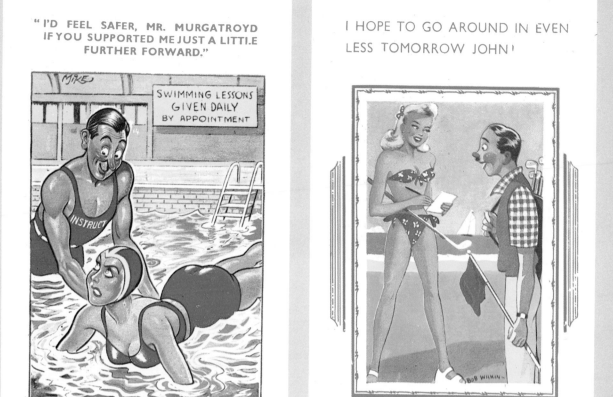

12052 "Would you like to stroke it, Miss Game?"

THE CAD

PUT ME AMONGST THE GIRLS

Taking a mean advantage.

"I'M JUST A BIT FAST"

WALTON-on-the-NAZE.

I could stay here for ever an' ever!

"A girl doesn't have to watch the speedometer to know what a man's DRIVING AT!"

I hope you've found SOMETHING INTERESTING TO LOOK AT while you're waiting, Mr Binks?

ACKNOWLEDGEMENTS

The author and publishers wish to thank the following for permission to reproduce cards in this book: D. Constance, Sapphire Publications, Mirror Group Newspapers for 'What a War' by Gilbert Wilkinson, Basil Buckland for the New Donald McGill Series, and Bamforth Marketing Company.

Every effort has been made to trace the copyright holders. If there should be any omissions, we apologise and shall be pleased to make the appropriate acknowledgement in future editions.

I would like to thank David Pearlman of 'Postcard Collectors Gazette', Basil Buckland and Michael Steyn for their special help, and Richard Chopping and Patrick Hughes for lending me their unique collections.

G.H.